# VICTOR SHMUD TOTAL EXPERT

## Let's Do a Thing!

## DON'T MISS THESE OTHER
# JIM BENTON
## TITLES:

Franny K. Stein #1–7

Dear Dumb Diary Year One #1–12

Dear Dumb Diary Year Two #1–6

## AND DON'T MISS . . .

Dear Dumb Diary, Deluxe:
Dumbness Is a Dish Best Served Cold

# VICTOR SHMUD TOTAL EXPERT

## Let's Do a Thing!

BOOK ONE

JIM BENTON

SCHOLASTIC PRESS / NEW YORK

This book is being published simultaneously in paperback by Scholastic Inc.



Library of Congress Cataloging-in-Publication Data available

ISBN 978-0-545-93233-2

10 9 8 7 6 5 4 3 2 1 17 18 19 20 21

Printed in the U.S.A. 23

First edition, June 2017

Book design by Jim Benton

Thanks to Kristen LeClerc,
Abby McAden, Yaffa Jaskoll,
and Kerianne Okie

Never, ever, ever lose your confidence.

# TABLE OF CONTENTS

# VICTOR SHMUD TOTAL EXPERT

## Let's Do a Thing!

# CHAPTER 1

## HELLO, VICTOR

Victor Shmud lived with his parents in a house with trees and bushes outside, but none of those things you see in front of houses sometimes, like little statues or birdbaths or things like that.

Victor always thought their house would look better with a thing out front, and he felt that anybody walking past could tell right away that there was a space right there that needed a thing in it.

Victor's room was always messy, because even though he had decided to be many things in his life, like a Knuckle Doctor, a Hunter of Ghost Bears, and The Guy at the Restaurant Who Puts the Sugar in Those Little Envelopes, he hadn't decided to be A Guy Who Cleans Up Bedrooms yet.

It actually wasn't even on the list.

Victor rolled out of bed and checked his computer—the highly advanced Electro-Brain Three Million—which he had created by writing ELECTRO-BRAIN THREE MILLION on the side of a cardboard box, back when he was a Computer Scientist a couple of weeks ago.

The Electro-Brain Three Million didn't work as well as other computers for email and going online, but it was square-shaped, and Victor believed that this was a good start.

Victor looked down at Dumpylumps, the tiny duck that had been by his side since he was a baby.

"What are you?" Victor asked. "A chicken or something?"

"Quack," said Dumpylumps.

"You should have that cough looked at," Victor said. "As an Expert Bird Veterinarian, I need to tell you that healthy chickens don't make noises like that."

REALLY
COUNTS

# CHAPTER 2

## SHMUD AT SCHOOL

Victor walked into the classroom and took a seat at the teacher's desk at the front of the room.

His teacher, Mrs. Nozzleburp, smiled sweetly at him, with a smile that had very nearly the correct number of teeth in it.

"Victor," she said, "you know that this desk is for the teacher. The smaller desks are for the students."

"Then you better take a seat in one of them, Mrs. Nozzleburp—you great big beautiful doll—because I'm teaching the class today. And if you don't mind, please keep it down. I'm the kind of teacher who likes it nice and quiet."

Mrs. Nozzleburp raised her eyebrows. She was pretty old, and eyebrows were just about the heaviest thing she could raise.

“Very kind of you to offer to teach the class, Victor,” she said. “And maybe one day I’ll take you up on that.”

She led him gently to his desk.

“But today I think I’ll have to go ahead and teach the class. It’s kind of a rule that the principal has.”

For a brief moment, Victor decided to be the principal.

"The principal is like the boss of the school," he whispered to himself, but then he began to worry that the principal probably had to take all the teachers home every night and feed them and give them baths and put them to bed.

“That’s too much work,” he whispered. “That could mean hundreds of tub toys.”

Mrs. Nozzleburp taught the class some stuff with words and numbers and how they were really important for reasons that Victor was forgetting as fast as she said them.

"I'll bet I'm some kind of Champion Forgetter," he said to himself. And he wondered if being able to forget things at superhuman speed was useful.

Suddenly, it was time for recess, and Victor asked the question that we all find ourselves asking at times.

# CHAPTER 3

## YO, WHERE'S MY CHICKEN?

Dumpylumps was waiting on the play-ground sitting on the rock that Victor had decided was his office.

"There you are," Victor said. "Just the chicken I needed to speak with."

"Quack," Dumpylumps said, hoping that Victor would notice what a very unchicken-ish thing that was to say.

"Here we are, already halfway through the morning, and I still haven't made a decision about what thing I'm going to do."

Dumpylumps took out his little notebook and pretended that he was taking notes on what Victor said.

"I had a career as a teacher very briefly earlier this morning, but it turns out that it's a highly competitive field, and I was replaced by an older, much more attractive teacher.

"I wonder if the other teachers are jealous of Mrs. Nozzleburp's attractiveness," Victor said.

Dumpylumps shrugged uncomfortably. He had never thought of her that way, and the entire conversation seemed inappropriate, and probably against one of the rules.

"Yes . . . ," Victor said thoughtfully. "Attractiveness!"

Dumpylumps pretended to underline the word *attractiveness*, which he had pretended to write.

"This seems like a thing I should look into," Victor said boldly.

Dumpylumps closed his eyes tightly. He knew where this was going.

"LET'S DO A THING!" Victor shouted, and he thrust his fist in the air, hoping there would be some thunder or lightning or something.

"Ckkaackk," Dumpylumps said, trying to sound like lightning.

# CHAPTER 4
## THING DOING

The next morning, Victor marched down the stairs with a strong sense of purpose.

"Mom," Victor said, "it's time you knew that I'm a Makeover Expert."

"You mean like a person who does people's hair and makeup?"

"That's right," he said.

"Okay," she said. "When did you become one?"

"I don't remember," Victor said, snipping her large scissors in the air. "It began long ago. I guess it was probably five or six o'clock this morning."

"I see," she said.

"Mom, look—you're a vision of glamour from head to toe, but if you ever need a little dusting off, let me know, and my assistant and I will be there to lend our expert help."

Dumpylumps nodded. He waved a comb at her and winked.

"I'll need to borrow a whole big bag of your makeup and hairspray and stuff. There are a lot of teachers who are going to be thrilled that they finally have somebody who understands how gross they are, and is willing to help them."

"You'll need to do what you can with just the comb," Mom said, taking the scissors away from him. "That's really all an expert needs anyway."

"You're not completely right, Mom," he said. "And I know that because I also happen to be an expert on knowing when people aren't completely right."

He slipped the comb into his pocket and headed off for the kitchen.

"Don't worry about the scissors. I don't need them. I can use common kitchen ingredients to make a spectacular beauty treatment," Victor said to Dumpylumps, who was at that very moment wondering to himself if he should just fly away and never come back.

"Some people have no idea how beneficial mustard can be in a shampoo. You know what's in it?" Victor asked as he combined various items from the refrigerator.

“Mustard molecules,” he whispered quietly, as if he was revealing a closely guarded secret. “The very essence of beauty.”

Victor headed off to school with Dumpylumps following behind him.

“It’s really amazing, isn’t it?”

Dumpylumps nodded. Most things amazed him—the universe, invisibility, peanut butter.

“Think about the great things we’ll be doing for people today,” Victor said, shaking his little bottle of beauty treatment.

# CHAPTER 5

## SAFE AND EFFECTIVE WHEN USED AS DIRECTED

The janitor at Victor's school was Mr. Plumporski, and he was a very hard worker. The kids made a lot of messes, and Victor made more than his fair share.

There was that time when Victor was an Octopus Wrestler, and Mr. Plumporski had to mop up the seawater he spilled.

And one time he was a Tattoo Artist and Mr. Plumporski had to scrub the tattoos off everybody.

And just last week, when Victor was a Wedding Planner and accidentally married some of the teachers to each other, it was Mr. Plumporski who had to help them get unmarried.

Victor knew he made a lot of work for Mr. Plumporski, and he felt it was only fair that he treated the janitor to the first makeover.

"Mr. Plumporski, how would you like to be beautiful?" Victor asked him as he pulled his little bottle from his backpack.

"What's *that* supposed to mean?" Mr. Plumporski said. "I'm already beautiful."

Mr. Plumporski posed in several beautiful poses to prove it.

"That's true, but this will make you beautifuller," Victor said, and he jumped up on the recycling bin and sprinkled some of his beauty preparation on Mr. Plumporski's head.

"It tingles," Mr. Plumporski said. "And *beautifuller* isn't a word."

"We hear new words every single day, Mr. Plumporski. Somebody has to make them. I happen to be a Licensed Wordmaker. It's what we do."

He showed him his official Wordmaker license.

Mr. Plumporski's hair started to curl. And then his eyebrows, and then his mustache.

"Look!" Victor shouted. "It's the curly hair that you always wanted."

"Yeah, I never said I wanted that! When will it stop? It's starting to hurt!"

"Soon. It will stop soon," Victor said. "Or never. Maybe never. You shouldn't have put so much on."

"You're the one who put it on me!"

As Victor and Dumpylumps walked away, Mr. Plumporski stuck his head in his mop bucket and washed off the beauty treatment.

Victor shook his finger at Dumpylumps.

"We need to label this stuff so that people don't get overly enthusiastic and use too much like Mr. Plumporski did," Victor said. "Not everybody is lucky enough to have a mop bucket nearby to dunk their heads in."

Dumpylumps nodded.

"You know, I always felt I'd be pretty good with a mop. Write that down as a thing I might do someday."

# CHAPTER 6

## SPACED OUT

Victor stared out the window as Mrs. Nozzleburp taught the class about the solar system.

"Victor," she said gently, "please pay attention."

"Don't worry. I heard everything you said, Mrs. Nozzleburp, and I can confirm that you've been absolutely correct about it all. You're doing a great job," Victor said, adding, "So far."

"Yes, thank you," she said. "But I need you to look up at the board."

She pointed at the lesson and her arm creaked under the weight of the marker.

Victor did as she asked. He worried that it would hurt her feelings if she thought he wasn't interested.

At recess, Victor sat on his rock with Dumpylumps and watched some kids play on the swings.

"Do you think any of those kids need surgery?" Victor asked him. "I could do some surgery things if they needed some."

Dumpylumps shrugged.

Victor had begun planning some surgery when his friend Patti walked up.

"Can I share your rock?" she asked. "The ground is wet."

"Sure," Victor said, lifting Dumpylumps aside to make room for her. "But we're preparing to perform surgery, so please don't distract us."

Dumpylumps scowled. He didn't like losing his seat.

Patti nodded and pulled her phone from her pocket. She started playing a game that made loud explosion sounds. She quickly turned down the volume.

"What's that?" Victor asked.

"It's a game called *Interspace Destruction Warriors*. You have to come up with the best strategy to defeat the alien enemy. It's really hard. I haven't been able to do it."

"I could have a look at it, if you like," Victor offered. "I'm an expert in Interspace Battle Strategy."

Dumpylumps sighed. He wanted his seat back.

At that very moment, in a large, battered spaceship very far away, a light on the control panel started to blink.

It was a ship belonging to the alien race called the Grooglings.

An alien named Sergeant Skulgo pushed some buttons and studied a screen full of maps of various solar systems. He called to the captain of the ship.

"Sir, our scanners have picked up what you've been looking for. We've found an expert in Interspace Battle Strategy. It's a human on a planet called Earth."

Captain Grulf's antennae twitched.

"Good work," he said. "Head there immediately."

# CHAPTER 7

## POOF

Victor studied the screen on Patti's phone and mashed randomly at the buttons.

"My strategies aren't working," he said. "I'm sorry, Patti, but this probably means your phone is broken."

"My phone is fine. You're just no better at it than I am." She laughed.

"Maybe the game loaded incorrectly," Victor said. "We'll have to have a look at the program itself."

Patti stood up and Victor set her phone down.

"Recess is almost over," she said.

Dumpylumps, finally spotting a place to sit, hopped up on the rock and accidentally sat on her phone.

He wiggled around to get comfortable and then was quite surprised to hear a muffled robot-type voice coming from underneath him.

"You win," the game said, and Dumpylumps smiled. He had never had somebody talk to his butt before.

Victor lifted him up.

"You won?" Patti asked, amazed.

"Yes," Victor said. "You see? I'm an expert."

He waved the phone triumphantly at Patti just as a beam crackled down from the sky and struck him.

Instantly, both he and Dumpylumps vanished in a little cloud of greenish smoke.

# CHAPTER 8

## THE GROOGLINGS

Victor and Dumpylumps were suddenly standing in front of a group of frowning aliens, aboard their battered spaceship.

"THIS is the strategy expert?" one of them growled as he scowled at Victor.

"That's what the scanners indicated," Sergeant Skulgo said. "Our data says that he defeated an enemy in a very difficult simulation."

"That's true, but my recess is almost over," Victor said. "And I need to get back to my school. There might be a birthday today, and as I'm sure you know, that *could* mean cupcakes."

Captain Grulf stepped forth.

"Human Victor, our scanners recorded you saying that you are an expert in Interspace Battle Strategy. Is that true?"

Victor thought for a moment.

"That is basically true," he said. "But I have also recently become a surgeon."

The aliens nodded at one another. A *surgeon*. They were impressed. One stepped up quietly behind Victor.

He showed Victor his arm. "Does this look infected?" he asked.

"Maybe he'll look at all of our infections later," Captain Grulf barked. "But right now, we need to get him and this duck creature to the battle station at once."

"It's a chicken," Victor said.

"Okay," Captain Grulf said. He knew what it was but didn't feel like arguing.

Back on Earth, the kids came in from recess and took their seats. Mrs. Nozzleburp made sure everybody was there.

"Does anybody know where Victor is?" she asked. "Is he in the bathroom?"

Patti raised her hand.

"Mrs. Nozzleburp, what's a word for when something is completely gone? Like, it was blown into a jillion tiny pieces?"

"Do you mean like *disintegrated* or *vaporized* or *pulverized*?" Mrs. Nozzleburp asked.

"I think I mean vaporized," Patti said. "Yes. It's vaporized."

Patti started coloring a picture at her desk.

"Oh. Wait," she said, stopping for a moment. "I wanted to tell you that Victor was vaporized." She smiled and went back to coloring her picture.

# CHAPTER 9

## THE FRAPPLETONIANS

The aliens sat Victor down in front of a huge control panel covered in buttons, dials, and keyboards.

"You guys probably think this is pretty complicated, don't you?" Victor asked them.

They wiggled their antennae at one another.

"So what if we do?" one said.

"It's just that it's not that complicated. I have one of these in my room. I got it when I was a baby."

"You did NOT get one of these when you were a baby," Sergeant Skulgo hissed.

"We can argue about my baby toys or I can just save the day and you can take me home," Victor said.

A voice came over the speaker system.

"Incoming Frappletonian fleet. Arrival time in five minutes."

Captain Grulf barked out the orders.

"Everybody to your positions. Human Victor, you better know what you're doing or the enemy will annihilate this ship."

"I hope they don't," Victor said. "That's where I am."

"That's where we *all* are. And our enemies, the Frappletonians, won't stop until they're destroyed, or we are."

Back in the classroom, Mrs. Nozzleburp sat limply in her chair. She had almost fainted and was trying to catch her breath.

"What do you mean, *he was vaporized*?" she wheezed.

Patti set down her crayon.

"Well, we were sitting on his rock, he was playing my game, lightning hit him, and . . . OH NO!"

"What?? What is it, Patti?"

"He has my phone!"

Onboard the spaceship, Captain Grulf spoke quietly to Victor.

"We've been at war with the Frappletonians for centuries. Every day. Every minute. They're unspeakably cruel. We must defeat them."

"How bad could they be?" Victor asked.

"How bad? Just for an example, have a look at this. We found a copy of their Things to Do for Fun Chart. When they're bored, they just pick one thing from every column, put them together, and do that thing."

He handed Victor the list.

# THE FRAPPLETONIANS'

## THINGS TO DO FOR FUN CHART

JUST PICK ONE THING FROM EACH COLUMN AND THEN **DO IT**

| COLUMN 1 | COLUMN 2 | COLUMN 3 | COLUMN 4 |
|---|---|---|---|
| KIDNAP | GRANDPA | AND POST A VIDEO OF | HIS BUTT |
| SPIT AT | SOME CHICKEN | AND TELL LIES ABOUT | HIS BAD HABITS |
| PINCH | A TINY BABY | AND TEASE HIM ABOUT | HIS GRANDMA'S BUTT |
| YELL MEAN WORDS AT | SICK PUPPY | AND WRITE A HIT SONG ABOUT | WHEN HE CRIES AT MOVIES |
| SPANK | THE PRINCIPAL | AND FORCE HIM TO ADMIT EVERYTHING ABOUT | HOW HE DOESN'T WASH HIMSELF WELL |

Victor shook his head.

"Okay. These guys *are* jerks," Victor said. "I understand. I'll do my best."

Mrs. Nozzleburp took out her phone and frantically dialed Patti's number.

Up on the alien ship, Victor answered.

"Hello. Victor Shmud speaking."

"Victor!" Mrs. Nozzleburp exclaimed. "I'm so happy to hear your voice. Where are you? What are you doing?"

"Oh, hi, Mrs. Nozzleburp. I'm just getting ready to do a battle thing with this spaceship I'm in. I'm helping some aliens fight the Frappletonians," he said. "What are you doing? Missing me like crazy, I'll bet."

"VICTOR! YOU MARCH RIGHT BACK HERE AND TAKE A SEAT AT YOUR DESK!" she demanded.

"No can do," he whispered. "These Frappletonians are pretty mean to grand-pas. I better help these guys out first."

He held the phone close to his mouth and whispered.

"And don't yell at me in front of these aliens. It's embarrassing."

"Victor," she said calmly, "the principal does not allow students to have space battles during the school day. Come back here at once."

"I'm sure that he'd permit THIS space battle," Victor said. "These Frappletonians might tell lies about his butt."

And he hung up.

# CHAPTER 10

## YOU SHOULD HAVE THAT SPOT LOOKED AT

"We got cut off! I have to call him back!" Mrs. Nozzleburp shouted. Her face turned red and she trembled like a small, wet dog.

"But he's right in the middle of something," Patti said. "Let's wait for him to call us. Or maybe we could call his duck. Is it legal for a duck to own a phone?"

Mrs. Nozzleburp frantically pressed the buttons to call Victor again.

Back up on the spaceship, the Grooglings were preparing for battle.

"Captain!" Sergeant Skulgo yelled, his antennae whipping madly around his head. "The enemy ship is coming in around the planet called Mars. We'll be within range in just a few minutes. Victor has control of the ship now."

"Understood, Sergeant. Are you paying attention, Victor?" Captain Grulf asked urgently.

The phone rang.

"I have to take this call, Captain. It might be important," Victor said. He pressed a button on the phone. It was Mrs. Nozzleburp again.

"Victor! Tell me exactly where you are!" she shouted.

"Mars is kind of in front of me. I can see that planet with the Hula-Hoop in my rear-view mirror."

"You mean Saturn?"

"That's right, Mrs. Nozzleburp. It's Saturn. Good job."

"Hang up the phone!" Sergeant Skulgo wailed.

"I have to go, Beautiful. They really want to start getting attacked right away and I guess I'm holding them up."

"Enemy ships closing in on us, sir," Sergeant Skulgo said.

"Attacked?" Patti asked.

"Oh, hi, Patti. Do you have me on speakerphone?"

"Yes," Patti said. "Tell us about this attack."

"It's a big deal, I guess," Victor said. "There are enemy ships headed toward us from behind Mars. It's pretty annoying."

Patti looked up at the board and studied the lesson Mrs. Nozzleburp had been giving them.

"What color is the ship you're on?"

Victor turned to Captain Grulf.

"Hey, Captain? What color is this ship? Like green or something? I'll bet it's green."

"It's RED," he shouted. "The color of battle. Now will you please hang up?"

Victor winked at him.

"Patti, it's red. The color of apples."

"I said BATTLE, not APPLES. NOW HANG UP!"

"Victor," Patti said urgently, "you should be pretty close to Jupiter."

"Which one is Jupiter?"

"It's big and round and has a giant red spot on it."

"Sounds like my grandma," Victor said.

"Enemy ships in range in thirty seconds, sir."

Patti spoke slowly and clearly.

"Position the ship so that you're in front of the spot. You'll be a red ship on a red background. Maybe they won't notice you."

"Good thinking," Victor said, and he steered the ship the way Patti had described.

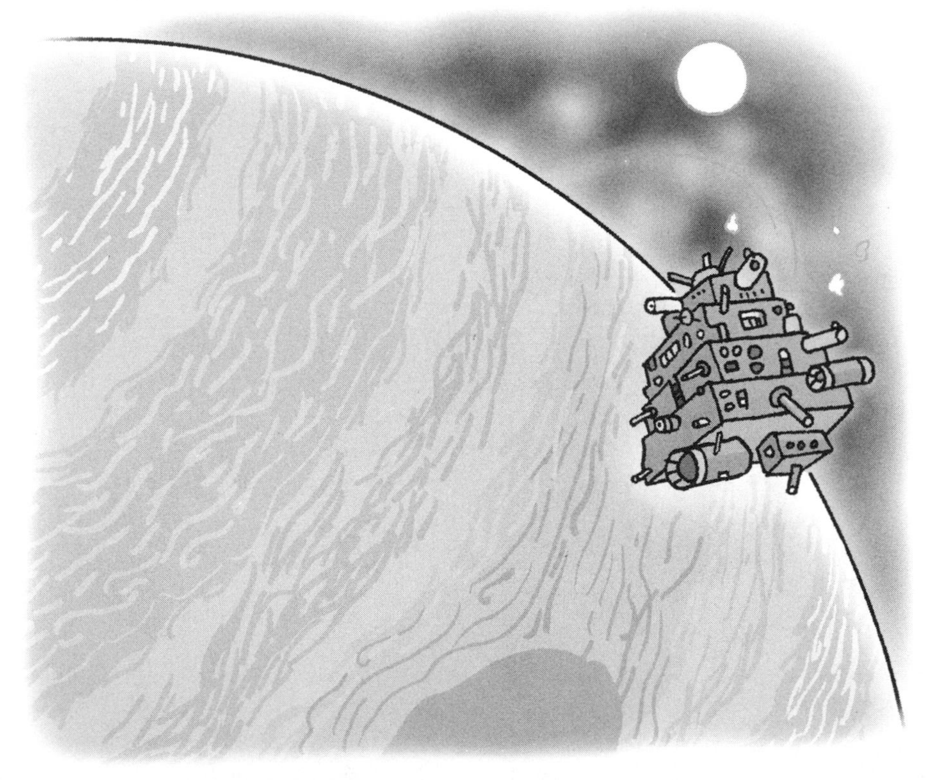

"Patti, I'll call you back. Unless we get blown up. If we get blown up, it won't be me calling."

Dumpylumps ran over to the wall and turned off the lights.

All of the aliens stopped talking and waited quietly in the dark as the massive Frappletonian ship slowly moved closer.

Sweat trickled down Captain Grulf's forehead. He held his breath.

The Frappletonian ship stopped for just a moment and then moved past them. The Frappletonians had not seen them. The plan had worked.

"Now we can attack them!" Sergeant Skulgo cried gleefully. "We'll get them from behind! They won't be prepared!"

"Maybe we shouldn't attack them," Victor said. "Maybe we could take a picture of them and send it to them and let them know that we COULD have attacked them, but we decided not to. You know, so that maybe you guys could start talking about peace."

Captain Grulf thought for a moment and nodded.

"This might be a good idea. Maybe we could try to have peace."

"This is ABSURD!" Sergeant Skulgo yelled, and he lunged for the control panel. His hand came down hard on a button, and before anybody could stop him, he had launched a missile.

# CHAPTER 11

## ALWAYS REMEMBER TO FORGET

Back in the classroom, Mrs. Nozzleburp's phone rang and Patti answered it.

"Whatcha doin'?" Patti asked.

"Oh, hi, Patti." Victor smiled. "Your plan worked great, but some guy here decided to start a battle anyway, so now the Frappletonians are super angry and we'll probably be blasted to bits. What are you doing?"

"Coloring," Patti said.

Laser blasts crashed into the Grooglings' ship. Victor pounded on the buttons, but nothing seemed to help. Some of the control panels burst into flames and Victor started to choke on the smoke.

Huge sections of the ship were breaking away, and the Groogling crew ran in all directions. Some began preparing to abandon ship.

"What are you coloring?" Victor asked.

"A duck. Like your duck."

"It's a chicken," Victor said firmly, and he picked up Dumpylumps.

"I have to go, Patti." He signed off, and hung up.

He stroked Dumpylumps's tiny head.

"We're in a pretty bad situation, Dumpylumps," Victor said, and Dumpylumps nodded sadly.

"It's over for us, you know," Victor said as he hugged Dumpylumps fiercely. "I love you, Dumpylumps."

Dumpylumps jumped up on the control panel and shook his butt at Victor.

"That's not a very nice thing to do," Victor said.

Dumpylumps picked up Patti's phone and waved it at him.

"Like the game! Of course!" Victor said, grabbing Dumpylumps.

Victor pounded Dumpylumps's butt on the control panel.

"If it worked in the game, it will work here!"

Dumpylumps's butt feathers flew as the Groogling ship whirled around and began firing at the Frappletonian ship. Like a skilled surgeon, Victor managed to shoot off only their guns, leaving the Frappletonians alive but unable to fire back.

He turned and spoke to Captain Grulf.

"The Frappletonians are helpless, sir."

"Attack them!" Sergeant Skulgo shouted. "Now! While they're at our mercy."

"You *could* do that," Victor said. "Or you could do something like we were discussing earlier. You could explain the situation to them. Tell them that you could destroy them, but that you would rather have peace."

"But how can we forget everything they've done to us?" Sergeant Skulgo hissed.

"You can forget *anything*. I forget stuff all the time. Nobody can remember everything," Victor said, happily poking him in the belly. "Just add all the stuff to the list of other things you've forgotten."

"Maybe it is time to forget," Captain Grulf said. "Yes. We'll try that, Victor, and this time, Sergeant Skulgo, DON'T INTERFERE!"

# CHAPTER 12

## THERE'S GOOD NEWS AND THERE'S BAD NEWS

### THE BAD NEWS IS THAT THERE REALLY ISN'T ANY GOOD NEWS

Mrs. Nozzleburp looked up at the sky as she listened nervously to Victor on her phone.

"I think we're just about done here, so I should be back any minute," he told her. "Hey, just for fun, put my boots out on the playground and I'll try to beam right into them."

"Victor, I know that you're not really in space, but I need you to return to class immediately. I'm really quite worried."

"I am in space. I can prove it," he said. "Wait, I'll send you a picture to prove it."

A photo came through on Mrs. Nozzleburp's phone. It was a picture of Dumpylumps.

"Did you get the picture I sent?" Victor asked.

"It's just a picture of your bird."

"Yeah, but it's a picture of him *in* space."

Captain Grulf put his big alien hands on Victor's shoulders.

"I have some great news," he said.

"Is it somebody's birthday?" Victor asked hopefully. "We're getting cupcakes, right?"

"No. We communicated with the Frappletonians. We explained everything, and we've all agreed to just forget the past and work toward peace."

"That's great," Victor said. "But you know, we could still ask around. There are a lot of crew members on this ship. It's probably somebody's birthday."

"We could not have done this without you, Victor."

"That's very nice of you to say, sir. I did have some help from this butt."

He held Dumpylumps up to the captain's face.

"Yes, we're all very grateful to that butt as well."

They all saluted Dumpylumps right in the butt.

"But here's the thing. If something like this comes up again, we're going to need you here. We've decided to make you a permanent crew member."

"That sounds pretty good," Victor said. "As long as I can do it from home, and not during school or on the weekends. Also, after school isn't so good for me. And I'm pretty busy in the summer."

Dumpylumps pulled out a calendar.

"Schedule something with my chicken here. We can make something work, I'm sure."

He winked at the captain.

"Now let's beam me back to the playground. Look for my boots and try to beam me right into them."

Captain Grulf snorted.

"First, that thing is a duck. And second, you don't have a choice in the matter," he said. "You are now a full-time member of this crew. You're never going back to Earth, and that's final. We need you here."

Victor was upset. He didn't mind being the battle expert on an interspace alien ship; in fact, he had planned to do that later on that month anyway. He just didn't like the idea that he wouldn't be able to do other things as well.

“Things are what I like best,” Victor murmured to Dumpylumps, who tried to remember all the things they had done just that week.

Victor frowned and secretly sent a text to Patti.

*Please send me picture of Nozzleburp,* it said.

# CHAPTER 13

## THE BEAUTY THAT IS NOZZLEBURP

Victor sat at the control panel and watched Earth get farther and farther away.

"I've thought about it, Captain Grulf, and I've decided that I'm looking forward to spending the rest of my horrible life as a prisoner on this busted-up and nasty alien ship."

“I’m glad to hear that, Victor. You may come to love this nasty ship.”

“I’m just sad that I’ll never get to see my beautiful Nozzleburp again.” Victor sniffed.

“What a lovely name,” Captain Grulf said. “Is she your mother?”

"My wife," Victor said sadly. "And she's the most beautiful woman on Earth."

He showed Captain Grulf the picture of Mrs. Nozzleburp that Patti had just texted him.

Captain Grulf's red eyes bulged and his mouth fell open.

"Hot bananas," he whispered. "She's gorgeous. From her woolly head to her majestically flapping elbow meat."

"Yes, she is," Victor said. "I made her that way."

"She's a robot?" Captain Grulf asked. Sergeant Skulgo and the other crew members handed the phone around to look at the picture.

"No, she's real. I said that I made her because I'm a beauty expert. It's just one of the things I do. I can do it for anybody."

Captain Grulf stroked his chin and leaned in close to Victor.

"Listen, Victor," he whispered. "I've always felt that I could use a little help in the looks department. Do you think you could make me a bit more handsome?"

"I could," Victor said. "But the kind of good looks I can give you could cause a problem on the ship. The whole crew would be jealous. It's a bad idea. We shouldn't do it."

Captain Grulf frowned.

"Wait. I have an idea," Victor said.

"What if you made us all beautiful? Then nobody would be jealous!"

He turned to his crew.

"How about it, guys? Do you all want to be beautiful? Beautiful like the Nozzleburp?"

They all cheered and began making very beautiful poses.

Victor quietly placed one more call home and talked to Patti.

"I need you to do a thing," he told her.

# CHAPTER 14

## IT'S NOT EASY BEING BEAUTIFUL

Captain Grulf, Sergeant Skulgo, and the rest of the Grooglings sat patiently and waited for Victor to begin. They clapped their gross hands in excitement.

"Please prepare yourself to be magnificent," he told them, and Dumpylumps held up a little sign to make sure they didn't forget.

"I will now apply my top-secret beauty treatment. It will make you unbelievably gorgeous and would probably also be pretty good on a sandwich, if one of you brought a sandwich."

Victor moved quickly down the line, sprinkling the substance on them the way he had used it on Mr. Plumporski.

"It tingles," one of them said.

"Interesting," Victor said. "It has the same effect on janitor heads."

"It's working," Captain Grulf shouted, and his antennae started to curl. And then his eyebrows, and then his whiskers.

"We're beautiful!" Sergeant Skulgo cheered, and they all admired one another's curls.

“Nice work,” Captain Grulf said. “You’re a great addition to the crew, and . . .” He stopped talking mid-sentence.

The other aliens clutched their antennae and started to whimper.

“It’s not stopping!”

“We’re curling too much!”

“It hurts!” they yelled.

“Victor! Make it stop!” Captain Grulf cried. He fell to the ground and rolled around in pain.

"I can't," Victor said. "The only stuff that will reverse this is on Earth, and you said we could never go back there. Sorry."

"Just go back!" Captain Grulf said. "Go now!"

Victor put on the turn signal and steered the ship around and headed back toward Earth.

"Hurry! We're becoming too beautiful!"

# CHAPTER 15

## MOPPING UP

Patti heard a loud screech, like the sound a school bus makes when it puts on the brakes. She looked out at the playground and saw the huge alien ship hovering over the ground.

The door opened and Victor waved.

"Is it okay to leave this ship here for a minute?" he shouted.

Mrs. Nozzleburp wobbled out to the playground.

"Victor! Come out of there!" she yelled.

"Okay, but I have to get these guys out first."

Victor operated the controls and began shaking the ship up and down until the weeping Grooglings spilled out onto the ground.

He then tossed Dumpylumps out of the ship and climbed down carefully onto Sergeant Skulgo's face.

"Patti, did you bring my equipment?" he asked.

"I did," she said, and handed him Mr. Plumporski's filthy mop.

"I always felt that I'd be pretty good with this thing," he said, and he dunked it in the mop bucket.

Victor carefully applied the mop to their faces and washed off some of the beauty treatment.

"I'm leaving just enough on for you to keep these flattering waves," Victor said. "You guys really applied too much. You shouldn't have used so much."

He turned to Dumpylumps.

"I thought I told you we needed a warning label on the bottle. You're fired."

Dumpylumps immediately fainted.

"Oh, get up," Victor said. "You're rehired. But I'm not going to pay you as much."

Dumpylumps thought for a moment, and realized that he had never been paid in the first place.

# CHAPTER 16

## ALL GOOD THINGS MUST COME TO AN END

Victor walked into his bedroom, followed by Dumpylumps.

"I guess we managed to do a thing today," Victor said. "And if you can do one of those every day, I think you're doing all right."

Dumpylumps nodded and put what was left of the beauty treatment up onto Victor's Special Shelf of Things.

"Remember to put a warning label on that. Put that on your to-do list. First, learn to write, then second, make that label," Victor instructed.

“It was a good idea that Patti had, making the Grooglings promise to keep peace with the Frappletonians,” Victor said. “She told them that I could reactivate those beautiful curls by remote. I can’t, of course, but they don’t know that.”

Dumpylumps tried to give a thumbs-up, but he wasn’t sure he even had a thumb.

“And I was glad that Mrs. Nozzleburp didn’t agree to marry the captain. One day, when I’m old enough, I plan to marry that big beautiful doll myself.”

Dumpylumps imagined what he would like to wear to the wedding.

Victor checked to see if his mustache had grown yet. He planned to propose to Mrs. Nozzleburp the moment it came in.

"Patti was a big help today," Victor said. "I'm thinking about giving her a permanent position on the rock."

Dumpylumps spun around and eyed him angrily. He did NOT want Patti to have a permanent position on their rock.

He threw his little notebook angrily to the floor and stood in the corner.

“Patti thought you should have this,” Victor said.

Dumpylumps was mad, but couldn’t resist turning his head slightly to see.

Victor opened a box and showed it to him. It was a rock.

“This will go right next to mine,” he said. “Look. Patti painted something on it.”

It said MR. DUMPYLUMPS, EXECUTIVE DUCK, and she had taped the picture she had drawn of him next to it.

His very own rock.

"I know what you're thinking. I told her over and over that you're a chicken, but she insisted that this is exactly what it should say."

Dumpylumps hugged Victor, and the two of them looked out the window.

A broken laser cannon that Victor had shot off the Frappletonian ship had fallen to Earth and landed right on his front lawn, where it smoldered and sparked.

"I always thought that would be a good spot for a thing," he said.

Dumpylumps nodded, and took a seat on his own personal rock. He picked up his little notebook and pretended to write something down.

Victor looked at him and grinned.

"Good week so far, Mr. Dumpylumps," he said. "Let's take a look at my calendar so you can tell me if I have a thing scheduled for tomorrow."

Join Victor and be an EXPERT at anything You want!
HAVING A REALLY GOOD BEARD
DENTISTRY FOR SPIDERS
STINKIGAMI (ORIGAMI WITH DIAPERS)
BEING MOSTLY INVISIBLE
oui oui
KNOWING WHICH FRENCH WORDS SOUND FUNNY.
HAVING A REALLY TERRIBLE BEARD
Wanting to do a thing is the most important part of things.

FROM VICTOR SHMUD #2:
VICTOR WEARS KINDERGARTNERS AS
BASKETBALL SHOES!